Walt Disney's
101 DALMATIANS

A Christmas "For-Giving"

By Elizabeth Spurr
Illustrations by DRI Artworks

One winter evening, Pongo, Perdita, and their ninety-nine puppies, walked into the parlor and found . . . a huge tree! It was fresh and green and made the room smell like a pine forest.

"What's going on?" the puppies asked their mother, looking slightly alarmed.

"Don't worry, dears," said Perdy. "This is just the beginning of Christmas."

Roger and Anita began acting very strangely. They were climbing on stepladders, hanging shiny, colored balls on the tree limbs, and arguing about the decorations. Should the treetop have a star, or an angel?

At last, the tree was decorated. The shiny ornaments cast a magical glow about the room.

That night, when Pongo and Perdita tucked the puppies into their baskets, they explained all about Christmas. It was a time when two-legged creatures like Roger and Anita showed their families and friends how much they cared for them.

"On Christmas Eve, after everyone's in bed," said Perdy, "people sneak presents under the tree for those they love."

"Because," said Pongo, "Christmas is about giving."

"Will we get presents?" asked Rolly.

"Maybe," Perdy replied. "I remember Anita gave me a new collar last year."

"And I got a red ball," said Pongo.

"I hope someone loves us," said Penny.

"Don't worry," said Perdy. "You are loved."

On Christmas morning the puppies woke at dawn. They crept into the living room. Sure enough, there were piles of brightly wrapped packages under the tree.

"We *are* loved!" cried Freckles. They all dove into the piles, tossing and ripping and tearing. Unwrapping was so much fun!

Lucky pulled open a box. His jaw dropped. "Perfume?"

Penny dragged a spotted necktie from the tissue paper. "Now, what do I need with more spots?" she said.

Freckles, looking downcast, held up a lace handkerchief.

And when Patch nosed out a satin nightgown, Lucky cried, "Uh-oh!"

The rest of the puppies chorused, "Uh-oh!"

Just then they heard Roger's and Anita's voices in the hallway.

"Out of here!" said Rolly. All ninety-nine puppies scampered away, hiding behind sofas, under chairs, or in the folds of the curtains.

Roger and Anita came into the parlor.

"What on earth?" Roger cried.

"Oh, dear!" Anita exclaimed.

Roger called, "Perdy, Pongo. Where are you?"

The puppies heard their parents run into the room. In their hiding places, the puppies trembled. They were in for it now!

Then, like music, came Anita's peal of laughter.

And Roger said, with a chuckle, "Looks like we've had some help opening our gifts."

After a pause, Anita said, "Wasn't that kind of the puppies!"

"Let's call them in," said Roger, "and say thanks. Here, puppies. Come here, pups!"

The puppies looked at one another. Should they answer?

Anita said in a loud voice, "There are still so many boxes to unwrap. I do wish they'd come and help."

One by one the puppies came into view, first creeping, then bounding. *Yip, yip, yip!*

As Roger pulled packages out from under the tree, the puppies gathered around. "Go for it, boys and girls!" he cried.

With happy barks, the puppies tore into the bright wrappings—the tangled ribbon, the crunchy cardboard, the crinkly papers. Pongo and Perdy watched amusedly as a snowstorm of wrapping flew through the air.

When all the gifts had been opened and all the papers set ablaze in the fireplace, Anita brought out a large basket. "Sorry we didn't have time to wrap these. But then," she said with a smile, "maybe you've done enough work for today."

She handed each puppy a squeaky toy. From the bottom of the basket she drew out two new collars for Pongo and Perdy.

That night, Perdy tucked the pups into their baskets. "We like Christmas!" said Pepper.

"Remember I told you that Christmas was about giving?" asked Perdy.

"We remember," said the puppies.

"It's also about *for*-giving," said Pongo gently. "You were lucky that Roger and Anita had the Christmas spirit."

The puppies looked at him, puzzled.

"From now on, there will be no more unwrapping—unless you have permission. Can you remember that?" asked Perdy.

And the puppies did remember.

At least, until Christmas came again.